Percy Bysshe Shelley

The Skylark, and Adonais

With Other Poems

Percy Bysshe Shelley

The Skylark, and Adonais
With Other Poems

ISBN/EAN: 9783337048020

Printed in Europe, USA, Canada, Australia, Japan

Cover: Foto ©Andreas Hilbeck / pixelio.de

More available books at **www.hansebooks.com**

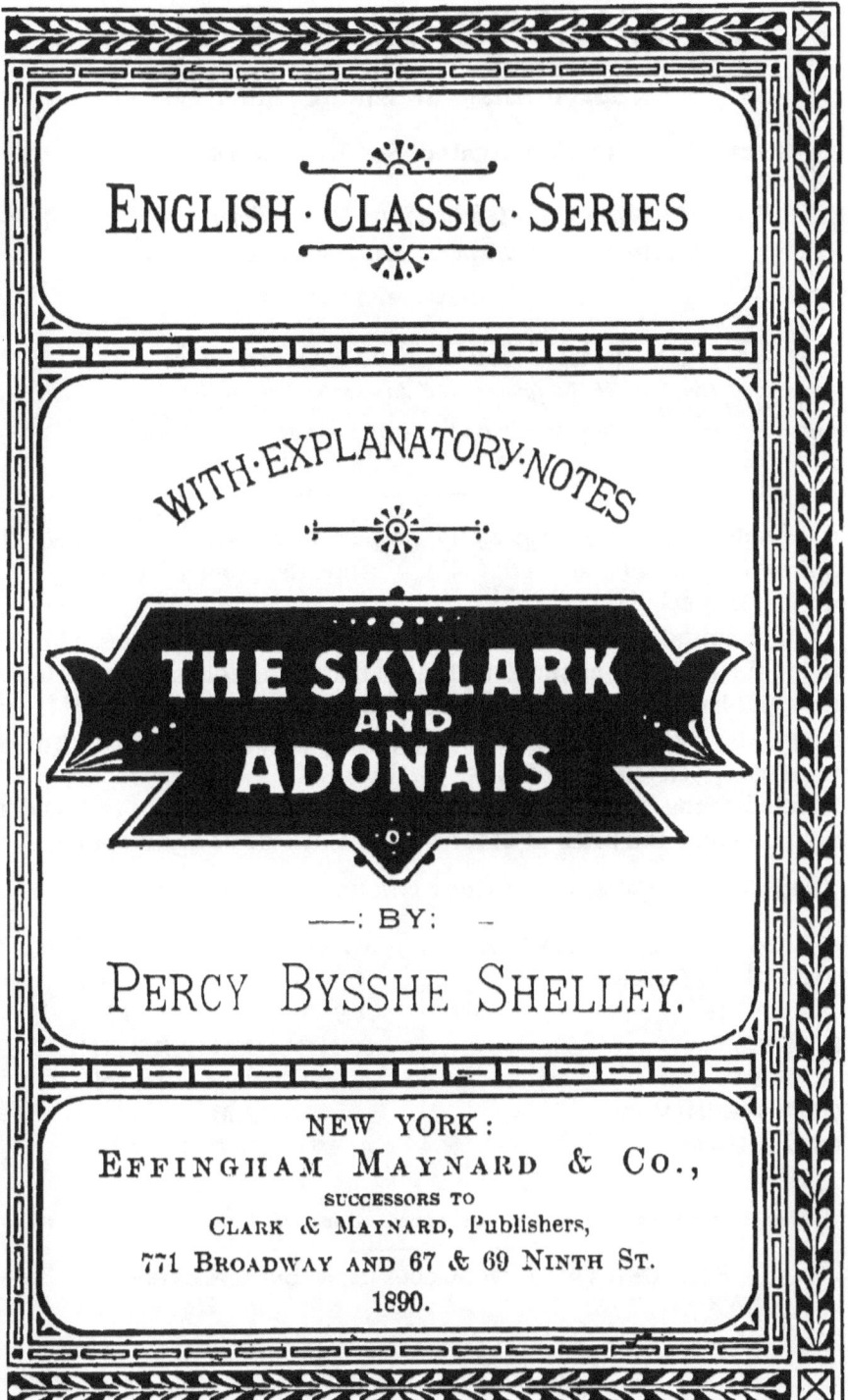

ENGLISH · CLASSIC · SERIES

WITH · EXPLANATORY · NOTES

THE SKYLARK AND ADONAIS

—: BY: —

PERCY BYSSHE SHELLEY.

NEW YORK:
EFFINGHAM MAYNARD & CO.,
SUCCESSORS TO
CLARK & MAYNARD, Publishers,
771 BROADWAY AND 67 & 69 NINTH ST.
1890.

SHAKESPEARE'S PLAYS.

Each play in One Volume.

Text Carefully Expurgated for Use in Mixed Classes.

With Portrait, Notes, Introduction to Shakespeare's Grammar, Examination Papers, and Plan of Study.

(SELECTED.)

By BRAINERD KELLOGG, A.M.,

Professor of the English Language and Literature in the Brooklyn Polytechnic Institute, and author of a "Text-Book on Rhetoric," a "Text-Book on English Literature," and one of the authors of Reed & Kellogg's "Lessons in English."

The notes have been especially prepared and selected, to meet the requirements of School and College Students, from editions by eminent English scholars.

We are confident that teachers who examine these editions will pronounce them better adapted to the wants of the class-room than any others published. **These are the only American Editions of these Plays that have been carefully expurgated for use in mixed classes.**

Printed from large type, attractively bound in cloth, and sold at nearly one half the price of other School Editions of Shakespeare.

The following Plays, each in one volume, are now ready:

MERCHANT OF VENICE.	KING HENRY IV., Part I.
JULIUS CÆSAR.	KING HENRY VIII.
MACBETH.	AS YOU LIKE IT.
TEMPEST.	KING RICHARD III.
HAMLET.	A MIDSUMMER-NIGHT'S
KING HENRY V.	DREAM.
KING LEAR.	A WINTER S TALE.

Mailing price, 30 cents per copy. Special Price to Teachers.

FULL DESCRIPTIVE CATALOGUE SENT ON APPLICATION.

THE SKYLARK AND ADONAIS.

WITH OTHER POEMS.

THE SKYLARK.
INTELLECTUAL BEAUTY.
STANZAS. WRITTEN IN DEJECTION,
    NEAR NAPLES.
THE CLOUD.
ARETHUSA.
HYMN OF APOLLO.

ODE TO THE WEST WIND.
THE QUESTION.
A SONG.
THE POET'S WORLD.
TO WORDSWORTH.
ADONAIS: AN ELEGY ON THE DEATH
    OF JOHN KEATS.

BY

PERCY BYSSHE SHELLEY.

With Introduction and Explanatory Notes

By J. W. ABERNETHY, Ph.D.,

PROFESSOR OF ENGLISH LITERATURE IN THE ADELPHI ACADEMY, BROOKLYN.

NEW YORK:

EFFINGHAM MAYNARD & CO., PUBLISHERS,

771 BROADWAY AND 67 & 69 NINTH STREET.

A COMPLETE COURSE IN THE STUDY OF ENGLISH.

Spelling, Language, Grammar, Composition, Literature.

Reed's Word Lessons—A Complete Speller.
Reed & Kellogg's Graded Lessons in English.
Reed & Kellogg's Higher Lessons in English.
Kellogg's Text-Book on Rhetoric.
Kellogg's Text-Book on English Literature

In the preparation of this series the authors have had one object clearly in view—to so develop the study of the English language as to present a complete, progressive course, from the Spelling-Book to the study of English Literature. The troublesome contradictions which arise in using books arranged by different authors on these subjects, and which require much time for explanation in the school-room, will be avoided by the use of the above " Complete Course."

Teachers are earnestly invited to examine these books.

EFFINGHAM MAYNARD & Co., Publishers,

771 Broadway, New York.

Introduction.

PERCY BYSSHE SHELLEY was born at Field Place, near Horsham in Sussex, August 4, 1792. He was the eldest of six children and the heir to a baronetcy. His father, Sir Timothy Shelley, was a wealthy country gentleman, proud of his lineage, and unfortunately possessed of a moral austerity that early brought him into disastrous conflict with his wildly-inspired son. The poet's early years were spent at Field Place with his four sisters; when ten years old, he was sent to a private academy, and two years later to Eton. He learned the classic languages "almost by intuition," and astonished his friends with the fluency of his Latin versification; his chief delight, however, was physical science, a taste for which he long retained. He devoured the extravagant romances of the period, and recorded indefinitely the flights of his own imagination in juvenile verses and tales. His desire for knowledge was insatiable; he possessed a remarkable power of memory, and read with astonishing rapidity. "No student ever read more assiduously. He was to be found, book in hand, at all hours; reading in season and out of season; at table, in bed, and especially during a walk; not only in the quiet country, and in retired paths; not only at Oxford, in the public walks, and High Street, but in the most crowded thoroughfares of London."

At Eton Shelley was unpopular. The qualities that separated him from the world in after life were early manifested—extreme sensitiveness, delicacy of tastes, impulsive and tender feelings, hatred of shams and conventions, intolerance of authority, and uncompromising hostility to tyranny and injustice in every form. "He was all passion," says Mrs. Shelley, "passionate in his resistance to an injury, passionate in his love." He organized a rebellion against the odious fagging system, and the brutal sports of his foot-ball loving companions, so generally deemed essential to manliness, aroused in him only the enthusiasm of disgust. Naturally enough, he was called "Mad Shelley."

At Oxford he was equally singular in his conduct and studies.

3

He showed a marked distaste for mathematics; was keenly interested in the principles involved in great political questions, but could not endure the trivial newspaper details of party warfare. Poetry and metaphysics mainly occupied his attention, and out of these he was already constructing that ideal, Platonic scheme of society unfolded in his early poems, by which broken humanity should be restored through universal truth, beauty, and love. Locke, Hume, and the French materialists were favorite authors at this time; under their influence, and as a means of indulging his passion for controversy, he issued a two-page pamphlet, entitled "The Necessity of Atheism," containing a series of propositions, so stated as to invite answers, embodying the main arguments of Hume and other rationalists against the existence of a Deity. The publication of this pamphlet led to his summary expulsion from the university, March 25, 1811. His father, with just indignation that the fair fame of his house should be sullied by an atheistical son, but with unjust coldness, closed the doors of Field Place upon the wilding, and the young poet-philosopher was forced suddenly to exchange his luxurious Oxford life of reading and dreaming for a struggle with poverty and the "many-headed beast" in London. Neither discomfort nor danger ever taught Shelley wisdom, in the worldly sense; with characteristic rashness he soon married a beautiful girl of sixteen, the daughter of a retired inn keeper, with nothing to depend upon but unwritten poems and a small annual allowance reluctantly granted by his father. Undaunted by the persecution of circumstances, and "resolving to lose no opportunity to disseminate truth and happiness," he at once set up as a reformer by writing and circulating pamphlets on Catholic Emancipation in Ireland, and a "Declaration of Rights," concerning the ends of government and the rights of man.

Shelley was a child of the French Revolution, and the victim of its intellectual excesses. He did not, like Wordsworth, free himself from the baneful influences of that first vision of "Liberty, Equality, Fraternity" that so dazzled the intellect of the new generation throughout Europe. His passionate devotion to liberty and his absorbing faith in a golden age of justice and peace, led him into the propagation of wild and obnoxious theories; and the consequent extravagance of expression often concealed the real man of noble impulse behind it. For this reason some of his earlier poems, as "Queen Mab" and "The Revolt of Islam," are almost unreadable, and, at publication, aroused only bitter hostility. But the freer utterance of the later lyrics reveals a soul filled with love, faith, and spiritual exaltation. He used the term "atheism," he said, "to express his abhorrence of superstition; he took it up as a knight took up a gauntlet in defiance of injustice." He might well have said with Schiller, "I have no religion, because of my religion." He loved mystery, loved to remain "hidden in the light of thought," and could not restrain his thinking by definition. "Lift not the painted veil," he cries, "which those that live call life." His spirit felt itself to be a part of the illimitable spirit of the universe. "He was not an atheist or a materialist," says Stopford Brooke. "If he may be said to have occupied any theoretical position, it was that of an Ideal Pantheist; a position which, with regard to Nature, a modern poet who cares for the subject, naturally—whatever may be his personal view—adopts in the realm of his art."

Before Shelley was eighteen he had published two novels, "Zastrozzi" and "The Rosicrucian," both incoherent medleys of sentiment, suggesting only remotely the future poet. In 1813 his first important poem, "Queen Mab," was printed. "Alastor," the finest of the long poems, was published in 1816. The best of the longer poems that followed are: "Julian and Maddalo," the transcendental love-poem, "Epipsychidion," and "The Witch of Atlas," "a poem in which he sent his imagination out, like a child into a meadow, without any aim save to enjoy itself." His finest poetry was produced in the last two years of his life, when he was no longer the reformer of mankind, but the isolated poet described in the exquisite allegory of the "Sensitive Plant." His "Prometheus Unbound" is a splendid lyrical drama on the subject of the Æschylean tragedy "Prometheus Bound;" and the "Cenci" is regarded as the most powerful drama written since the age of Elizabeth. The fragmentary prose works contain much that is beautiful; few passages can be found in English prose equal to the essay entitled "A Defense of Poetry."

Soon after the death of his first wife, in 1816, Shelley married Mary Godwin, the gifted daughter of William Godwin, the author of "Caleb Williams." In March, 1818, after an alarming illness, he went to Italy, where the brief remainder of his life was spent. Here in the companionship of a few choice friends, and in reposeful enjoyment of the lofty skies and purple fields, the broad visions of beauty, the romantic witchery of this land of poetry, his genius found its best and truest inspiration. Here he had just begun to show with what sustained ease and consummate art he could rise to the loftiest reaches of inspired song, when his voice was suddenly silenced. His last residence was the Casa Magni, on the Bay of Spezia, where he indulged much in his favorite sport of boating. On the afternoon of July 8, 1822, while returning from a visit of welcome to Leigh Hunt at Leghorn, his frail yacht was capsized in a gale and all on board perished. Shelley's body was washed ashore a few days later and, in accordance with the quarantine regulations, was burned by his friends Byron, Trelawney, and Leigh Hunt, and the ashes deposited in the Protestant cemetery at Rome, near the grave of Keats —that spot he had just described so beautifully in " Adonais." In view of the achievement of the life thus brought to an untimely end, it may well be called " a miracle of thirty years."

Shelley is " the most poetical of poets since the days of Elizabeth," says Stopford Brooke. Of his proper rank, the poet Swinburne ventures the opinion " that of all forms or kinds of poetry the two highest are the lyric and the dramatic, and that as clearly as the first place in the one rank is held among us by Shakespeare, the first place in the other is held and will never be resigned by Shelley." Says J. Addington Symonds : " In none of Shelley's greatest contemporaries was the lyrical faculty so paramount ; and whether we consider his minor songs, his odes, or his more complicated choral dramas, we acknowledge that he was the loftiest and the most spontaneous singer of our language. In range of power he was also conspicuous above the rest. Not only did he write the best lyrics, but the best tragedy, the best translations, and the best familiar poems of his century."

Professor Shairp, who estimates the poet's character and genius with true Scotch conservatism, says of the lyrics: " Single thrills of rapture, which are insufficient to make long poems out of, supply the very inspiration for the true lyric. It is this predominance of emotion, so unhappy to himself, which made Shelley the lyrist that he was. When he sings his lyric strains, whatever is least pleasing in him is softened down, if it does not wholly disappear. Whatever is most unique and excellent in him comes out at its best—his eye for abstract beauty, the subtlety of his thought, the rush of his eager pursuing desire, the splendor of his imagery, the delicate rhythm, the matchless music. These lyrics are gales of melody blown from a far-off region, that looks fair in the distance. To enjoy them it may perhaps be as well not to inquire too closely what is the nature of that land, or to know too exactly the theories and views of life of which these songs are the effluence." The critic and the poet's biographer, W. M. Rossetti, thus summarizes his work: " He excels all his competitors in ideality, he excels them in music, and he excels them in importance. By importance we here mean the direct import of the work performed, its controlling power over the reader's thought and feeling, the contagious fire of its white-hot intellectual passion, and the long reverberation of its appeal. We have named ideality as one of his leading excellencies. This Shelleian quality combines, as its constituents, sublimity, beauty, and the abstract passion for good. It should be acknowledged that, while this great quality forms the chief and most admirable factor in Shelley's poetry, the defects that go along with it mar his work too often—producing at times vagueness, unreliability, and a pomp of glittering indistinctness, in which excess of sentiment welters amid excess of words. The blemish affects the long poems much more than the pure lyrics; in the latter the rapture, the music, and the emotion are in exquisite balance, and the work has often as much of delicate simplicity as of fragile and flower like perfection."

Keen as are
the ~~Shy notes like~~ the snows
Of that silver sphere,
Whose intense lamp narrows
In the white dawn clear
Until we hardly see — we feel that it is there;

2

Higher still & higher
From the earth thou springest
Like a cloud of fire
The blue deep thou wingest
And singing ~~still~~ dost soar & soaring ever singest
     and

All the earth & air —
With thy voice is loud,
As when Night is bare
From one lonely cloud
The moon rains out her beams — & Heaven is overflowed

What thou art we know not
What is most like thee?
From ~~thy~~ rainbow clouds there flow not
Drops so bright to see
As from thy presence showers a rain of melody

Fac-simile of Manuscript Page of Skylark.

8

THE SKYLARK AND ADONAIS.

To a Skylark.

This ode, the most popular and the most perfect of Shelley's lyrics, was written in the poet's twenty-ninth year, two years before his death. This poem and the "Cloud," says Mrs. Shelley, "were written as his mind prompted, listening to the carolling of the bird, aloft in the azure sky of Italy, or marking the cloud as it sped across the heavens, as he floated in his boat on the Thames." "Describing the song of a skylark," says Prof. De Mille, "may be compared to an artist's attempt to paint a rainbow ; yet in this attempt Shelley has not failed. He has tested to the uttermost the capacities of language, and has exhausted its resources in this wonderful ode. It is penetrated through and through with the spirit of the beautiful, and has more of high and pure poetic rapture than any other ode in existence." Wordsworth's "To a Skylark" and "To the Cuckoo" should be read with this poem for comparison.

HAIL to thee, blithe spirit !
Bird thou never wert,
That from heaven, or near it,
Pourest thy full heart
In profuse strains of unpremeditated art.　　　　　5

Higher still and higher
From the earth thou springest
Like a cloud of fire ;
The blue deep thou wingest,
And singing still dost soar, and soaring ever singest.　　10

---

3. So Shakespeare begins the morning song for Imogen, in "Cymbeline:"
"Hark, hark ! the lark at heaven's gate sings."
8. Prof. Craik maintains that the semi-colon should be after "springest," for the prosaic reason that "a cloud does not spring from the ground." This marking obviously would not give the poet's meaning. The lark is already high up in the sky and in the second stanza he is mounting "higher still," continuously, and swiftly like fire. (See *Fac-simile*). Compare Procter's lines in "Invocation to Birds," describing the lark's flight :
"Sky-climbing bird, wakener of morn,
Who springeth like a thought unto the sun."

9

In the golden lightning
Of the sunken sun,
O'er which clouds are brightning,
Thou dost float and run ;
Like an unbodied joy whose race is just begun.   15

The pale purple even
Melts around thy flight ;
Like a star of heaven,
In the broad day-light
Thou art unseen, but yet I hear thy shrill delight,   20

Keen as are the arrows
Of that silver sphere,
Whose intense lamp narrows
In the white dawn clear,
Until we hardly see, we feel that it is there.   25

All the earth and air
With thy voice is loud,
As, when night is bare,
From one lonely cloud
The moon rains out her beams, and heaven is   30
          overflowed.

What thou art we know not ;
What is most like thee ?
From rainbow clouds there flow not
Drops so bright to see,
As from thy presence showers a rain of melody.   35

---

15. **Unbodied:** Many editions have "embodied," an "emendation" de-
fended by Prof. Craik. Upon this Prof. Baynes comments thus : " To the
swift sympathetic imagination of the poet, the scorner of the ground, floating far up in the golden light, had become an ærial rapture, a disembodied
joy, a 'delighted spirit,' whose ethereal race had just begun. This is a rep-
resentation at once profoundly poetical and profoundly true. But its force
and consistency are destroyed by the so-called emendation." The MS. copy
of the poem gives *unbodied.*
20. Compare Tennyson's " In Memoriam," cxv.:
          " And drowned in yonder living blue
          The lark becomes a sightless song."
21-25. In the poem " Evening " we have the "keen evening star," and in
the " Cloud " the morning star " shines dead." Ruskin speaks of the long
avalanches "cast down in *keen* streams brighter than the lightning."
31-32. The poet, unable to tell *what* this ethereal creature is, whether
"sprite or bird," now tells what is most *like* this "blithe spirit" in a series

Like a poet hidden
  In the light of thought,
Singing hymns unbidden,
  Till the world is wrought
To sympathy with hopes and fears it heeded not :   40

Like a high-born maiden
  In a palace tower,
Soothing her love-laden
  Soul in secret hour
With music sweet as love, which overflows her bower : 45

Like a glow-worm golden
  In a dell of dew,
Scattering unbeholden
  Its aërial hue
Among the flowers and grass, which screen it from   50
      the view :

Like a rose embowered
  In its own green leaves,
By warm winds deflowered,
  Till the scent it gives
Makes faint with too much sweet these heavy-wingèd 55
      thieves :

Sound of vernal showers
  On the twinkling grass,
Rain-awakened flowers,
  All that ever was
Joyous, and clear, and fresh, thy music doth surpass : 60

Teach us, sprite or bird,
  What sweet thoughts are thine :
I have never heard
  Praise of love or wine
That panted forth a flood of rapture so divine.   65

---

of similes of unapproachable beauty. A comparison of this lyric with James
Hogg's "Skylark" is interesting as showing the difference between an inspired and an uninspired poet.

  64. **Praise of love or wine**: Lyrical poetry in general, as love and
wine are the most common subjects of song.

Chorus Hymenæal,
    Or triumphal chaunt,
Matched with thine would be all
    But an empty vaunt,
A thing wherein we feel there is some hidden want.   70

What objects are the fountains
    Of thy happy strain ?
What fields, or waves, or mountains?
    What shapes of sky or plain ?
What love of thine own kind ? what ignorance of pain ? 75

With thy clear keen joyance
    Languor cannot be :
Shadow of annoyance
    Never came near thee :
Thou lovest ; but ne'er knew love's sad satiety.   80

Waking or asleep,
    Thou of death must deem
Things more true and deep
    Than we mortals dream,
Or how could thy notes flow in such a crystal stream ! 85

We look before and after,
    And pine for what is not :
Our sincerest laughter
    With some pain is fraught ;
Our sweetest songs are those that tell of saddest   90
        thought.

Yet if we could scorn
    Hate, and pride, and fear ;
If we were things born
    Not to shed a tear,
I know not how thy joy we ever should come near.   95

---

80. " The sound of this lovely line," says Rossetti, " would be so spoiled by changing the word into ' knew'st,' that no rectification of grammar is permissible."

90. Poe makes this thought a principle, applicable to all art; "Let me remind you that(how or why we know not) this certain taint of sadness is insepably connected with all the higher manifestations of true beauty."

Better than all measures
Of delightful sound,
Better than all treasures
That in books are found,
Thy skill to poet were, thou scorner of the ground !   100

Teach me half the gladness
That thy brain must know,
Such harmonious madness
From my lips would flow,
The world should listen then, as I am listening now.   105

------◆------

Hymn to Intellectual Beauty.

This poem was written in 1816. It expresses the poet's earliest aspirations
and epitomizes his philosophy of life—consecration to the service of ideal
truth, love, and beauty. Its fundamental idea is that of Plato's "supreme
beauty," explained in the "Banquet," which Shelley translated. It has
much in common with Wordsworth's great ode on the "Intimations of Immortality," both in the thought and in the rhythm.

THE awful shadow of some unseen Power
   Floats tho' unseen amongst us,—visiting
   This various world with an inconstant wing
As summer winds that creep from flower to flower,—
Like moonbeams that behind some piny mountain shower, 5
      It visits with inconstant glance
      Each human heart and countenance;
Like hues and harmonies of evening,—
      Like clouds in starlight widely spread,—
      Like memory of music fled,—   10
      Like aught that for its grace may be
Dear, and yet dearer for its mystery.

---

1. **Awful**: This word, as used throughout the poem in the sense of *awe-inspiring*, significantly expresses the intensity of Shelley's feeling.

Spirit of BEAUTY, that dost consecrate
  With thine own hues all thou dost shine upon
  Of human thought or form,—where art thou gone?   15
Why dost thou pass away and leave our state,
This dim vast vale of tears, vacant and desolate?
    Ask why the sunlight not forever
    Weaves rainbows o'er yon mountain river,
Why aught should fail and fade that once is shown, '   20
    Why fear and dream and death and birth
    Cast on the daylight of this earth
    Such gloom,—why man has such a scope
For love and hate, despondency and hope?

No voice from some sublimer world hath ever   25
  To sage or poet these responses given—
  Therefore the names of Demon, Ghost, and Heaven,
Remain the records of their vain endeavor,
Frail spells—whose uttered charm might not avail to sever,
    From all we hear and all we see,   30
    Doubt, chance, and mutability.
Thy light alone—like mist o'er mountains driven,
    Or music by the night wind sent,
    Thro' strings of some still instrument,
    Or moonlight on a midnight stream,   35
Gives grace and truth to life's unquiet dream.

Love, Hope, and Self-esteem, like clouds depart
  And come, for some uncertain moments lent.
  Man were immortal and omnipotent,
Didst thou, unknown and awful as thou art,   40
Keep with thy glorious train firm state within his heart.
    Thou messenger of sympathies,
    That wax and wane in lovers' eyes—
Thou—that to human thought art nourishment,
    Like darkness to a dying flame!   45
    Depart not as thy shadow came,
    Depart not—lest the grave should be,
Like life and fear, a dark reality.

While yet a boy I sought for ghosts, and sped
   Thro' many a listening chamber, cave and ruin,   50
   And starlight wood, with fearful steps pursuing
Hopes of high talk with the departed dead.
I called on poisonous names with which our youth is fed,
    I was not heard—I saw them not—
    When musing deeply on the lot   55
Of life, at that sweet time when winds are wooing
    All vital things that wake to bring
    News of birds and blossoming,—
    Sudden, thy shadow fell on me ;
I shrieked, and clasped my hands in ecstasy !   60

I vowed that I would dedicate my powers
   To thee and thine—have I not kept the vow ?
   With beating heart and streaming eyes, even now
I call the phantoms of a thousand hours   [65
Each from his voiceless grave : they have in visioned bowers
    Of studious zeal or love's delight
    Outwatched with me the envious night—
They know that never joy illumined my brow
    Unlinked with hope that thou wouldst free
    This world from its dark slavery,   70
    That thou—O awful LOVELINESS,
Wouldst give whate'er these words cannot express.

The day becomes more solemn and serene
   When noon is past—there is a harmony
   In autumn, and a lustre in its sky,   75
Which thro' the summer is not heard or seen,
As if it could not be, as if it had not been !

50, 51. See note on the rhyme *ruin, pursuing*, p. 23, ll. 52, 53.
61. In the dedication to " Revolt of Islam " is another description of the awakening of his spirit to its sublime mission. Similarly Wordsworth says of himself, in describing his early aspirations :

               "I made no vows, but vows
    Were made for me ; bond unknown to me
    Was given, that I should be, else sinning greatly,
    A dedicated spirit."

Thus let thy power, which like the truth
Of nature on my passive youth
Descended, to my onward life supply   80
   Its calm—to one who worships thee,
   And every form containing thee,
   Whom, SPIRIT fair, thy spells did bind
To fear himself, and love all human kind.

The Cloud.

I BRING fresh showers for the thirsting flowers,
   From the seas and the streams;
I bear light shade for the leaves when laid   .
   In their noon-day dreams.
From my wings are shaken the dews that waken   5
   The sweet buds every one,
When rocked to rest on their mother's breast,
   As she dances about the sun.
I wield the flail of the lashing hail,
   And whiten the green plains under,   10
And then again I dissolve it in rain,
   And laugh as I pass in thunder.

I sift the snow on the mountains below,
   And their great pines groan aghast;
And all the night 'tis my pillow white,   15
   While I sleep in the arms of the blast.
Sublime on the towers of my skiey bowers,
   Lightning my pilot sits,
In a cavern under is fettered the thunder,
   It struggles and howls at fits;   20
Over earth and ocean, with gentle motion,
   This pilot is guiding me,
Lured by the love of the genii that move
   In the depths of the purple sea;

---

82. The repetition of *thee*, instead of making a rhyme, was undoubtedly intended for emphasis.

Over the rills, and the crags, and the hills,   25
  Over the lakes and the plains,
Wherever he dream, under mountain or stream,
  The Spirit he loves remains ;
And I all the while bask in heaven's blue smile,
  Whilst he is dissolving in rains.   30

The sanguine sunrise, with his meteor eyes,
  And his burning plumes outspread,
Leaps on the back of my sailing rack,
  When the morning star shines dead,
As on the jag of a mountain crag,   35
  Which an earthquake rocks and swings,
An eagle alit one moment may sit
  In the light of its golden wings.
And when Sunset may breathe, from the lit sea beneath,
  Its ardors of rest and of love,   40
And the crimson pall of eve may fall
  From the depth of heaven above,
With wings folded I rest, on mine airy nest,
  As still as a brooding dove.

That orbèd maiden with white fire laden,   45
  Whom mortals call the moon,
Glides glimmering o'er my fleece-like floor,
  By the midnight breezes strewn,
And wherever the beat of her unseen feet,
  Which only the angels hear,   50
May have broken the woof of my tent's thin roof,
  The stars peep behind her and peer ;
And I laugh to see them whirl and flee
  Like a swarm of golden bees,
When I widen the rent in my wind-built tent,   55
  Till the calm rivers, lakes, and seas,
Like strips of the sky fallen through me on high,
  Are each paved with the moon and these.

---

33. **Rack:** An old word, still used in northern England for light, broken, vapory clouds in motion ; as in "The Tempest," iv. 1, "like this insubstantial pageant faded, leave not a rack behind."

I bind the sun's throne with a burning zone,
    And the moon's with a girdle of pearl ;   60
The volcanos are dim, and the stars reel and swim,
    When the whirlwinds my banner unfurl.
From cape to cape, with a bridge-like shape,
    Over a torrent sea,
Sunbeam-proof, I hang like a roof,   65
    The mountains its columns be.
The triumphal arch through which I march
    With hurricane, fire and snow,
When the powers of the air are chained to my chair,
    Is the million-colored bow ;   70
The sphere-fire above its soft colors wove,
    While the moist earth was laughing below.

I am the daughter of earth and water,
    And the nursling of the sky ;
I pass through the pores of the ocean and shores ;   75
    I change, but I cannot die.
For after the rain when with never a stain,
    The pavilion of heaven is bare,
And the winds and sunbeams with their convex gleams,
    Build up the blue dome of air,   80
I silently laugh at my own cenotaph,
    And out of the caverns of rain,
Like a child from the womb, like a ghost from the tomb,
    I arise and unbuild it again.

77-84. Compare the following lines, written the next year (1821):

    "When soft winds and sunny skies
    With the green earth harmonize,
    And the young and dewy dawn,
    Bold as an unhunted fawn,
    Up the windless heaven is gone,—
    Laugh—for ambushed in the day,
    Clouds and whirlwinds watch their prey."

The Poet's World.

(From "Prometheus Unbound.")

On a poet's lips I slept
Dreaming like a love-adept
In the sound his breathing kept;
Nor seeks nor finds he mortal blisses,
But feeds on the aërial kisses
Of shapes that haunt thought's wildernesses.
He will watch from dawn to gloom
The lake-reflected sun illume
The yellow bees in the ivy bloom,
Nor heed nor see what things they be;
But from these create he can
Forms more real than living man,
Nurslings of immortality!

———◆———

Stanzas.

WRITTEN IN DEJECTION, NEAR NAPLES.

The sun is warm, the sky is clear,
  The waves are dancing fast and bright,
Blue isles and snowy mountains wear
  The purple noon's transparent might,
  The breath of the moist earth is light,   5
Around its unexpanded buds;
  Like many a voice of one delight,
The winds, the birds, the ocean floods,
The City's voice itself is soft like Solitude's.

I see the Deep's untrampled floor   10
   With green and purple seaweeds strown ;
I see the waves upon the shore,
   Like light dissolved in star-showers, thrown :
   I sit upon the sands alone,
The lightning of the noon-tide ocean   15
   Is flashing round me, and a tone
Arises from its measured motion,
How sweet ! did any heart now share in my emotion.

Alas ! I have nor hope nor health,
   Nor peace within nor calm around,   20
Nor that content surpassing wealth
   The sage in meditation found,
   And walked with inward glory crowned—
Nor fame, nor power, nor love, nor leisure.
   Others I see whom these surround—   25
Smiling they live, and call life pleasure ;—
To me that cup has been dealt in another measure.

Yet now despair itself is mild,
   Even as the winds and waters are ;
I could lie down like a tired child,   30
   And weep away the life of care
   Which I have borne and yet must bear,
Till death like sleep might steal on me,
   And I might feel in the warm air
My cheek grow cold, and hear the sea   35
Breathe o'er my dying brain its last monotony.

Some might lament that I were cold,
   As I, when this sweet day is gone,
Which my lost heart, too soon grown old,
   Insults with this untimely moan ;   40
   They might lament—for I am one
Whom men love not,—and yet regret,
   Unlike this day, which, when the sun
Shall on its stainless glory set,
Will linger, though enjoyed, like joy in memory yet. 45

Hymn of Apollo.

THE sleepless Hours who watch me as I lie,
   Curtained with star-inwoven tapestries,
From the broad moonlight of the sky,
   Fanning the busy dreams from my dim eyes,—
Waken me when their Mother, the gray Dawn,   5
Tells them that dreams and that the moon is gone.

Then I arise, and climbing Heaven's blue dome,
   I walk over the mountains and the waves,
Leaving my robe upon the ocean foam ;
   My footsteps pave the clouds with fire ; the caves   10
Are filled with my bright presence, and the air
Leaves the green earth to my embraces bare.

The sunbeams are my shafts, with which I kill
   Deceit, that loves the night and fears the day ;
All men who do or even imagine ill   15
   Fly me, and from the glory of my ray
Good minds and open actions take new might,
Until diminished by the reign of night.

I feed the clouds, the rainbows and the flowers
   With their æthereal colors ; the Moon's globe   20
And the pure stars in their eternal bowers
   Are cinctured with my power as with a robe ;
Whatever lamps on Earth or Heaven may shine,
Are portions of one power, which is mine.

I stand at noon upon the peak of Heaven,   25
   Then with unwilling steps I wander down
Into the clouds of the Atlantic even ;
   For grief that I depart they weep and frown :
What look is more delightful than the smile
With which I soothe them from the western isle ?   30

I am the eye with which the Universe
  Beholds itself and knows itself divine ;
All harmony of instrument or verse,
  All prophecy, all medicine are mine,
All light of art or nature ;—to my song,   35
Victory and praise in their own right belong.

Arethusa.

ARETHUSA arose
  From her couch of snows
In the Acroceraunian mountains,—
  From cloud and from crag,
  With many a jag,   5
Shepherding her bright fountains.
  She leapt down the rocks,
  With her rainbow locks
Streaming among the streams ;—
  Her steps paved with green   10
  The downward ravine
Which slopes to the western gleams :
  And gliding and springing
  She went, ever singing,
In murmurs as soft as sleep ;   15
  The Earth seemed to love her,
  And Heaven smiled above her,
As she lingered towards the deep.

  Then Alpheus bold,
  On his glacier cold,   20

---

1. **Arethusa** was a nymph of Arcadia, who, being pursued by the river-
god Alpheus, was changed into a stream by Diana; disappearing under
ground, she passed beneath the Ionian sea, and reappeared as a fountain
in the island of Ortygia. But the river-god, still pursuing, finally won her,
and they dwelt "single-hearted" in the fountains of Enna's mountains.
3. **Acroceraunian:** An epithet applied by the poets to several mountains
of Greece. From Gr. ἄκρον, peak, and κεραύνιος, thunder-smitten.

With his trident the mountains strook
    And opened a chasm
    In the rocks ;—with the spasm
All Erymanthus shook.
    And the black south wind   25
    It concealed behind
The urns of the silent snow,
    And earthquake and thunder
    Did rend in sunder
The bars of the springs below :   30
    The beard and the hair
    Of the River-god were
Seen through the torrent's sweep,
    As he followed the light
    Of the fleet nymph's flight   35
To the brink of the Dorian deep.

    "Oh, save me ! Oh, guide me!
    And bid the deep hide me,
For he grasps me now by the hair !"
    The loud Ocean heard,   40
    To its blue depth stirred,
And divided at her prayer ;
    And under the water
    The Earth's white daughter
Fled like a sunny beam ;   45
    Behind her descended
    Her billows, unblended
With the brackish Dorian stream :—
    Like a gloomy stain
    On the emerald main   50
Alpheus rushed behind,—
    As an eagle pursuing
    A dove to its ruin
Down the streams of the cloudy wind.

---

24. **Erymanthus:** A mountain of Arcadia, famous as the place where Hercules killed the wild boar.
36. **Dorian deep:** The Ionian sea. The Dorians originally occupied southern and western Peloponnesus; hence *Dorian* is often used for *Grecian.*
52, 53. Upon the awkward rhyme Forman says: "I cannot think that Shelley would have permitted himself to indulge in so indefensible a solecism

Under the bowers   55
Where the Ocean Powers
Sit on their pearlèd thrones,
Through the coral woods
Of the weltering floods,
Over heaps of unvalued stones ;   60
Through the dim beams
Which amid the streams
Weave a network of colored light ;
And under the caves,
Where the shadowy waves   65
Are as green as the forest's night :—
Outspeeding the shark,
And the sword-fish dark,
Under the ocean foam,
And up through the rifts   70
Of the mountain clifts
They past to their Dorian home.

And now from their fountains
In Enna's mountains,
Down one vale where the morning basks,   75
Like friends once parted
Grown single-hearted,
They ply their watery tasks.
At sunrise they leap
From their cradles steep   80
In the cave of the shelving hill ;
At noon-tide they flow
Through the woods below
And the meadows of Asphodel ;

---

had the words not formed a rhyme to him; and it seems likely that, being of the aristocratic caste, the habit of dropping the final *g* was indelibly acquired as a child and youth, and never struck him as a bad habit to be got over. If so, to him *ruin* and *pursuing* were a perfect rhymn."

60, **Unvalued stones:** Stones of inestimable value. Compare " Richard III.," I. 26:

> " Wedges of gold, great anchors, heaps of pearl,
> Inestimable stones, unvalued jewels,
> All scattered in the bottom of the sea."

So in Milton's sonnet, " On Shakespeare," " thy unvalued book."

84. **Asphodel:** A plant associated by the ancients with the dead. Its pale blossoms covered the meadows of Hades, where the ghosts of the dead were wont to roam in search of the waters of Lethe, or oblivion. Corrupted in English into *daffodil*.

And at night they sleep   85
In the rocking deep
Beneath the Ortygian shore ;—
Like spirits that lie
In the azure sky
When they love but live no more.   90

A Song.

A WIDOW bird sate mourning for her love
    Upon a wintry bough ;
The frozen wind crept on above,
    The freezing stream below.

There was no leaf upon the forest bare,
    No flower upon the ground,
And little motion in the air
    Except the mill-wheel's sound.

To Wordsworth.

POET of Nature, thou hast wept to know
That things depart which never may return :
Childhood and youth, friendship and love's first glow,
Have fled like sweet dreams, leaving thee to mourn.
These common woes I feel.   One loss is mine   5
Which thou too feel'st yet I alone deplore.
Thou wert as a lone star, whose light did shine
On some frail bark in winter's midnight roar :

1-5. The allusion in these lines is to Wordsworth's "Ode on the Intimations of Immortality."
    7. Compare Wordsworth's lines on Milton in the sonnet "London, 1802:"
"Thy soul was like a star, and dwelt apart."

Thou hast like to a rock-built refuge stood
Above the blind and battling multitude: 10
In honored poverty thy voice did weave
Songs consecrate to truth and liberty,—
Deserting these, thou leavest me to grieve,
Thus having been, that thou shouldst cease to be.

Ode to the West Wind.

"This poem," says Shelley, "was conceived and chiefly written in a wood that skirts the Arno, near Florence, and on a day when that tempestuous wind, whose temperature is at once mild and animating, was collecting the vapors which pour down the autumnal rains. They began, as I foresaw, at sunset, with a violent tempest of hail and rain, attended by that magnificent thunder and lightning peculiar to the Cis-alpine regions. The phenomenon alluded to at the conclusion of the third stanza is well known to naturalists. The vegetation at the bottom of the sea, of rivers, and of lakes, sympathizes with that of the land in the change of seasons, and is consequently influenced by the winds that announce it."

This poem alone, says Stopford Brooke, "is enough to place Shelley apart from the other lyric poets of England. There is no song in the whole of our literature more passionate, more penetrative, more full of the force by which the idea and its form are united into one creation."

I.

O, WILD West Wind, thou breath of Autumn's being,
Thou, from whose unseen presence the leaves dead
Are driven, like ghosts from an enchanter fleeing,

Yellow, and black, and pale, and hectic red,
Pestilence-stricken multitudes: O, thou,   5
Who chariotest to their dark wintry bed

The wingèd seeds, where they lie cold and low,
Each like a corpse within its grave, until
Thine azure sister of the spring shall blow

13–14. Wordsworth had abandoned the principles of the French Revolution, which he at first embraced with enthusiasm, and had gone back into the Tory fold. Shelley regarded him as a deserter from the cause of liberty. See Browning's "Lost Leader," which expresses the same feeling toward Wordsworth.

Her clarion o'er the dreaming earth, and fill   10
(Driving sweet buds like flocks to feed in air)
With living hues and odors plain and hill :

Wild Spirit, which art moving every where ;
Destroyer and preserver ; hear, O, hear !

II.

Thou on whose stream, 'mid the steep sky's commotion, 15
Loose clouds like earth's decaying leaves are shed,
Shook from the tangled boughs of Heaven and Ocean,

Angels of rain and lightning : there are spread
On the blue surface of thine airy surge,
Like the bright hair uplifted from the head   20

Of some fierce Mænad, even from the dim verge
Of the horizon to the zenith's height
The locks of the approaching storm.   Thou dirge

Of the dying year, to which this closing night
Will be the dome of a vast sepulcher,   25
Vaulted with all thy congregated might

Of vapors, from whose solid atmosphere
Black rain, and fire, and hail will burst :   O, hear !

III.

Thou who didst waken from his summer dreams
The blue Mediterranean, where he lay,   30
Lulled by the coil of his crystálline streams,

Beside a pumice isle in Baiæ's bay,
And saw in sleep old palaces and towers
Quivering within the wave's intenser day,

All overgrown with azure moss and flowers   35
So sweet, the sense faints picturing them !   Thou
For whose path the Atlantic's level powers

Cleave themselves into chasms, while far below
The sea-blooms and the oozy woods which wear
The sapless foliage of the ocean, know   40

Thy voice, and suddenly grow gray with **fear**,
And tremble and despoil themselves : O, hear !

IV.

If I were a dead leaf thou mightest bear ;
If I were a swift cloud to fly with thee ;
A wave to pant beneath thy power, and share   45

The impulse of thy strength, only less free
Than thou, O, uncontrollable ! If even
I were as in my boyhood, and could be

The comrade of thy wanderings over heaven,
As then, when to outstrip thy skiey speed   50
Scarce seemed a vision ; I would ne'er have striven

As thus with thee in prayer in my sore need.
Oh ! lift me as a wave, a leaf, a cloud !
I fall upon the thorns of life ! I bleed !

A heavy weight of hours has chained and bowed   55
One too like thee : tameless, and swift, and proud.

V.

Make me thy lyre, even as the forest is :
What if my leaves are falling like its own !
The tumult of thy mighty harmonies

Will take from both a deep, autumnal tone,   60
Sweet though in sadness.   Be thou, spirit fierce,
My spirit ! Be thou me, impetuous one !

Drive my dead thoughts over the universe
Like withered leaves to quicken a new birth !
And, by the incantation of this verse,   65

Scatter, as from an unextinguished hearth
Ashes and sparks, my words among mankind !
Be through my lips to unawakened earth

The trumpet of a prophecy ! O, wind,
If Winter comes, can Spring be far behind ?   70

The Question.

I DREAMED that, as I wandered by the way,
  Bare winter suddenly was changed to spring,
And gentle odors led my steps astray,
  Mixed with a sound of waters murmuring
Along a shelving bank of turf, which lay   5
  Under a copse, and hardly dared to fling
Its green arms round the bosom of the stream,
But kissed it and then fled, as thou mightest in dream.

There grew pied wind-flowers and violets,
  Daisies, those pearled Arcturi of the earth,   10
The constellated flower that never sets ;
  Faint oxlips; tender bluebells, at whose birth
The sod scarce heaved; and that tall flower that wets—
  Like a child, half in tenderness and mirth—
Its mother's face with heaven-collected tears,   15
When the low wind, its playmate's voice, it hears.

And in the warm hedge grew lush eglantine,
  Green cow-bind and the moonlight-colored May,
And cherry blossoms, and white cups, whose wine
  Was the bright dew, yet drained not by the day;   20
And wild roses, and ivy serpentine,
  With its dark buds and leaves, wandering astray;
And flowers azure, black, and streaked with gold,
Fairer than any wakened eyes behold.

And nearer to the river's trembling edge   25
  There grew broad flag-flowers, purple prankt with white,
And starry river buds among the sedge,
  And floating water-lilies, broad and bright,

---

10. Arcturi: Plural of *Arcturus*, the name of a beautiful star of the first
magnitude in the constellation Boötes, behind the Great Bear. In another
poem the daisy is " the daisy-star that never sets."

Which lit the oak that overhung the hedge
  With moonlight beams of their own watery light ;   30
And bulrushes, and reeds of such deep green
As soothed the dazzled eye with sober sheen.

Methought that of these visionary flowers
  I made a nosegay, bound in such a way
That the same hues, which in their natural bowers   35
  Were mingled or opposed, the like array
Kept these imprisoned children of the Hours
  Within my hand,—and then, elate and gay,
I hastened to the spot whence I had come,
That I might there present it !—oh ! to whom?   40

Adonais.

AN ELEGY ON THE DEATH OF JOHN KEATS.

Keats died at Rome, in 1820, in his twenty-fourth year. Shelley, then living
at Pisa, was profoundly moved by sorrow and indignation, and immediately
wrote this noble elegy, believing his brother poet's death to have been caused
by the attacks of ruffianly reviewers. "The genius of the lamented person
to whose memory I have dedicated these unworthy verses," he says, "was
not less delicate and fragile than it was beautiful; and where canker-worms
abound, what wonder if its young flower was blighted in the bud? The savage criticism on his 'Endymion,' which appeared in the Quarterly Review,
produced the most violent effect upon his susceptible mind."

"Adonais" is equalled in our language only by Milton's "Lycidas," to which
it is even superior in passionate eloquence. It should also be compared with
Tennyson's "In Memoriam" and Arnold's "Thyrsis." Shelley's own opinion of the poem has generally been shared by appreciative readers. "The
'Adonais.' in spite of its mysticism," he wrote to a friend, "is the least
imperfect of my compositions. It is a highly wrought *piece of art*, and
perhaps better, in point of composition, than anything I have written." In
alluding to the stanzas against the infamous Quarterly reviewer, he said: "I
have dipped my pen in consuming fire for his destroyers; otherwise the
style is calm and solemn."

I WEEP for Adonais—he is dead !
O, weep for Adonais ! though our tears

---

1 Adonais: The poet fancies a resemblance between the death of Keats
and that of Ado'nis, the beautiful youth, of Greek mythology, who was
gored to death by a wild boar in a hunt; hence *Adona'is.*

Thaw not the frost which binds so dear a head !
And thou, sad Hour, selected from all years
To mourn our loss, rouse thy obscure compeers,   5
And teach them thine own sorrow, say: with me
Died Adonais; till the Future dares
Forget the Past, his fate and fame shall be
An echo and a light unto eternity !

Where wert thou mighty Mother, when he lay,   10
When thy Son lay, pierced by the shaft which flies
In darkness? where was lorn Urania
When Adonais died ?   With veilèd eyes,
'Mid listening Echoes, in her Paradise
She sate, while one, with soft enamored breath,   15
Rekindled all the fading melodies,
With which, like flowers that mock the corse beneath,
He had adorned and hid the coming bulk of death.

O, weep for Adonais—he is dead !
Wake, melancholy Mother, wake and weep !   20
Yet wherefore?   Quench within their burning bed
Thy fiery tears, and let thy loud heart keep
Like his, a mute and uncomplaining sleep;
For he is gone, where all things wise and fair
Descend ;—oh, dream not that the amorous Deep   25
Will yet restore him to the vital air;
Death feeds on his mute voice, and laughs at our despair.

Most musical of mourners, weep again !
Lament anew, Urania !—He died,   ——
Who was the Sire of an immortal strain,   30
Blind, old, and lonely, when his country's pride,
The priest, the slave, and the liberticide,
Trampled and mocked with many a loathèd rite
Of lust and blood; he went, unterrified,
Into the gulf of death; but his clear Sprite   35
Yet reigns o'er earth; the third among the sons of light.

4. **Sad Hour:** The hour of the poet's death, whose fellow hours are "obscure" because they have witnessed no such great event for mourning.
12. **Urania:** The Muse of Astronomy. Shelley follows Milton in making her the muse of loftiest poetry, the true "Heavenly" muse, with voice "divine." See "Paradise Lost," bk. vii. 1-10.
29-33. The allusion is to Milton, and the reaction against the Puritan

Most musical of mourners, weep anew !
Not all to that bright station dared to climb;
And happier they their happiness who knew,
Whose tapers yet burn through that night of time   **40**
In which suns perished; others more sublime,
Struck by the envious wrath of man or God,
Have sunk, extinct in their refulgent prime;
And some yet live, treading the thorny road,
Which leads, through toil and hate, to Fame's serene abode.

But now, thy youngest, dearest one has perished,   **46**
The nursling of thy widowhood, who grew,
Like a pale flower by some sad maiden cherished,
And fed with true love tears, instead of dew;
Most musical of mourners, weep anew !   **50**
Thy extreme hope, the loveliest and the last,
The bloom, whose petals nipt before they blew
Died on the promise of the fruit, is waste;
The broken lily lies—the storm is overpast.

To that high Capital, where kingly Death   **55**
Keeps his pale court in beauty and decay,
He came; and bought, with price of purest breath,
A grave among the eternal.—Come away!
Haste, while the vault of blue Italian day
Is yet his fitting charnel-roof! while still   **60**
He lies, as if in dewy sleep he lay;
Awake him not ! surely he takes his fill
Of deep and liquid rest, forgetful of all ill.

He will awake no more, oh, never more!—
Within the twilight chamber spreads apace   **65**
The shadow of white Death, and at the door
Invisible Corruption waits to trace

---

struggle for liberty under Charles II. The other two "sons of light" are
probably Homer and Dante.

38-45. "Not all poets have essayed such lofty flights as Milton, i.e, at-
tempted epic poetry, but some have wisely taken a lower level, i.e., at-
tempted lyric poetry, and are still remembered as lyric poets, as for
instance Gray or Burns; others, attempting a middle flight, have been cut
off in the midst of their work, as Spenser; others yet live, of whom nothing
definite can yet be said, e.g., Shelley himself, and Byron."—*Prof. Hales.*

55. **High Capital:** Rome, the "lone mother of dead empires."

His extreme way to her dim dwelling-place;
The eternal Hunger sits, but pity and awe
Soothe her pale rage, nor dares she to deface   70
So fair a prey, till darkness, and the law
Of change, shall o'er his sleep the mortal curtain draw.

O, weep for Adonais!—The quick Dreams,
The passion-wingèd Ministers of thought,
Who were his flocks, whom near the living streams   75
Of his young spirit he fed, and whom he taught
The love which was its music, wander not,—
Wander no more, from kindling brain to brain,
But droop there, whence they sprung; and mourn their lot
Round the cold heart, where, after their sweet pain,   80
They ne'er will gather strength, or find a home again.

And one with trembling hands clasps his cold head,
And fans him with her moonlight wings, and cries;
"Our love, our hope, our sorrow, is not dead;
See, on the silken fringe of his faint eyes,   85
Like dew upon a sleeping flower, there lies
A tear some Dream has loosened from his brain."
Lost Angel of a ruined Paradise!
She knew not 'twas her own; as with no stain
She faded, like a cloud which had outwept its rain.   90

One from a lucid urn of starry dew
Washed his light limbs as if embalming them;
Another clipt her profuse locks, and threw
The wreath upon him, like an anadem,
Which frozen tears instead of pearls begem;   95
Another in her wilful grief would break
Her bow and wingèd reeds, as if to stem
A greater loss with one which was more weak;
And dull the barbèd fire against his frozen cheek.

Another Splendor on his mouth alit,   100
That mouth, whence it was wont to draw the breath

---

84. Compare "Lycidas," l. 166: "For Lycidas your sorrow is not dead."
99. As if she would dull the piercing fire of her heart-grief by contact with his death-cold cheek.

Which gave it strength to pierce the guarded wit,
And pass into the panting heart beneath
With lightning and with music: the damp death
Quenched its caress upon his icy lips;   105
And, as a dying meteor stains a wreath
Of moonlight vapor, which the cold night clips,
It flushed through his pale limbs, and past to its eclipse.

And others came . . . Desires and Adorations,
Wingèd Persuasions and veiled Destinies,   110
Splendors, and Glooms, and glimmering Incarnations
Of hopes and fears, and twilight Phantasies;
And Sorrow, with her family of Sighs,
And Pleasure, blind with tears, led by the gleam
Of her own dying smile instead of eyes,   115
Came in slow pomp;—the moving pomp might seem
Like pageantry of mist on an autumnal stream.

All he had loved, and molded into thought,
From shape, and hue, and odor, and sweet sound,
Lamented Adonais.   Morning sought   120
Her eastern watch-tower, and her hair unbound,
Wet with the tears which should adorn the ground,
Dimmed the aërial eyes that kindle day;
Afar the melancholy thunder moaned,
Pale Ocean in unquiet slumber lay,   125
And the wild winds flew round, sobbing in their dismay.

Lost Echo sits amid the voiceless mountains,
And feeds her grief with his remembered lay,
And will no more reply to winds or fountains,
Or amorous birds perched on the young green spray,   130
Or herdsman's horn, or bell at closing day;
Since she can mimic not his lips, more dear
Than those for whose disdain she pined away
Into a shadow of all sounds:—a drear
Murmur, between their songs, is all the woodmen hear.   135

---

107. Clips: Embraces, holds; from A. S *clyppan*, to embrace.
133. Echo was a nymph in love with *Narcissus*; but her love not being
returned, she pined away till only her voice remained.

Grief made the young Spring wild, and she threw down
  Her kindling buds, as if she Autumn were,
  Or they dead leaves ; since her delight is flown
For whom should she have waked the sullen year ?
To Phœbus was not Hyacinth so dear   140
  Nor to himself Narcissus, as to both
  Thou Adonais : wan they stand and sere
  Amid the faint companions of their youth,
With dew all turned to tears ; odor, to sighing ruth.

Thy spirit's sister, the lorn nightingale   145
  Mourns not her mate with such melodious pain ;
  Not so the eagle, who like thee could scale
Heaven, and could nourish in the sun's domain
Her mighty youth with morning, doth complain,
  Soaring and screaming round her empty nest,   150
  As Albion wails for thee : the curse of Cain
  Light on his head who pierced thy innocent breast,
And scared the angel soul that was its earthly guest !

Ah woe is me ! Winter is come and gone,
  But grief returns with the revolving year ;   155
  The airs and streams renew their joyous tone ;
The ants, the bees, the swallows reappear ;
Fresh leaves and flowers deck the dead Seasons' bier ;
  The amorous birds now pair in every brake,
  And build their mossy homes in field and brere ;   160
  And the green lizard, and the golden snake,
Like unimprisoned flames, out of their trance awake.

Through wood and stream and field and hill and Ocean
  A quickening life from the Earth's heart has burst
  As it has ever done, with change and motion,   165
From the great morning of the world when first

140–141. **Hyacinth** was a youth beloved by Phœbus, and killed by the
jealous Zephyr. From his blood sprang the flower, which bears upon its
petals the words *ai, ai*, alas! alas! *Narcissus*, having fallen in love with his
own reflection in a fountain, pined away and was at last changed to a
flower (see Cl. Dic.). The fancy is that the other flowers of spring, with the
Hyacinth and the Narcissus, droop and fade with grief.
145. An allusion, perhaps, to Keats' "Ode to the Nightingale."
160. **Brere**: Briar ; hence, as here, a thicket.

God dawned on Chaos ; in its steam immersed
The lamps of Heaven flash with a softer light ;
All baser things pant with life's sacred thirst ;
Diffuse themselves ; and spend in love's delight,   170
The beauty and the joy of their renewèd might.

The leprous corpse touched by this spirit tender
Exhales itself in flowers of gentle breath ;
Like incarnations of the stars, when splendor
Is changed to fragrance, they illumine death   175
And mock the merry worm that wakes beneath ,
Nought we know, dies.   Shall that alone which knows
Be as a sword consumed before the sheath
By sightless lightning ?—th' intense atom glows
A moment, then is quenched in a most cold repose.   180

Alas ! that all we loved of him should be,
But for our grief, as if it had not been,
And grief itself be mortal ! Woe is me !
Whence are we, and why are we? of what scene
The actors or spectators?   Great and mean   185
Meet massed in death, who lends what life must borrow.
As long as skies are blue, and fields are green,
Evening must usher night, night urge the morrow,
Month follow month with woe, and year wake year to
    sorrow.

He will awake no more, oh, never more !   190
"Wake thou," cried Misery, " childless Mother, rise
Out of thy sleep, and slake, in thy heart's core,
A wound more fierce than his with tears and sighs."
And all the Dreams that watched Urania's eyes,
And all the Echoes whom their sister's song   195
Had held in holy silence, cried : " Arise !"
Swift as a Thought by the snake Memory stung,
From her ambrosial rest the fading Splendor sprung.

---

177. **Knows :** That alone which possesses the power of knowing.
179. **Sightless lightning :** Invisible lightning.
191-193. Wake thou, Urania, and allay with tears and sighs the wound at
thy heart, more fierce than that which killed Adonais.
195. **Sister's song :** The Echo who "rekindled" the poet's melodies in
Urania's Paradise (l. 15).

She rose like an autumnal Night, that springs
Out of the East, and follows wild and drear   200
The golden Day, which, on eternal wings,
Even as a ghost abandoning a bier,
Had left the Earth a corpse. Sorrow and fear
So struck, so roused, so rapt Urania ;
So saddened round her like an atmosphere   205
Of stormy mist ; so swept her on her way
Even to the mournful place where Adonais lay.

Out of her secret Paradise she sped,
Through camps and cities rough with stone, and steel,
And human hearts, which to her aery tread   210
Yielding not, wounded the invisible
Palms of her tender feet where er they fell :
And barbèd tongues, and thoughts more sharp than they
Rent the soft Form they never could repel,
Whose sacred blood, like the young tears of May,   215
Paved with eternal flowers that undeserving way.

In the death chamber for a moment Death
Shamed by the presence of that living Might
Blushed to annihilation, and the breath
Revisited those lips, and life's pale light   220
Flashed through those limbs, so late her dear delight.
"Leave me not wild and drear and comfortless,
As silent lightning leaves the starless night !
Leave me not !" cried Urania : her distress
Roused Death : Death rose and smiled, and met her vain caress.

"Stay yet awhile ! speak to me once again ;   225
Kiss me, so long but as a kiss may live ;
And in my heartless breast and burning brain
That word, that kiss shall all thoughts else survive,
With food of saddest memory kept alive,   230
Now thou art dead, as if it were a part
Of thee, my Adonais ! I would give
All that I am to be as thou now art !
But I am chained to Time, and cannot thence depart !

" Oh gentle child, beautiful as thou wert,   235
Why didst thou leave the trodden paths of men
Too soon, and with weak hands though mighty heart
Dare the unpastured dragon in his den ?
Defenceless as thou wert, oh where was then
Wisdom the mirrored shield, or scorn the spear ?   240
Or hadst thou waited the full cycle, when
Thy spirit should have filled its crescent sphere,
The monsters of life's waste had fled from thee like deer.

" The herded wolves, bold only to pursue ;
The obscene ravens, clamorous o'er the dead ;   245
The vultures to the conqueror's banner true
Who feed where Desolation first has fed,
And whose wings rain contagion ;—how they fled,
When like Apollo, from his golden bow,
The Pythian of the age one arrow sped   250
And smiled !—The spoilers tempt no second blow,
They fawn on the proud feet that spurn them lying low.

" The sun comes forth, and many reptiles spawn ;
He sets, and each ephemeral insect then
Is gathered into death without a dawn,   255
And the immortal stars awake again ;
So is it in the world of living men :
A godlike mind soars forth, in its delight
Making earth bare and veiling heaven, and when
It sinks, the swarms that dimmed or shared its light   260
Leave to its kindred lamps the spirit's awful night."

Thus ceased she : and the mountain shepherds came,
Their garlands sere, their magic mantles rent ;

---

238. **Unpastured dragon** : The unfed dragon, i.e., the savage critic, the "monster of life's waste."
240. **Mirrored shield** : The shield of wisdom is a mirror in which folly sees its own face.
245. **Obscene** : Latin *obscenus*, of evil omen; hence repulsive, abominable.
249-250. Apollo slew the dragon Python at Delphi (see Cl. Dic.). The "Pythian of the age" was Byron, who sped his arrow at the whole brood of ravenous critics in his " English Bards and Scotch Reviewers."
259. " Lighting up the earth so brightly that it is not possible to see the stars."
263. Prospero, in the " Tempest," wears a " magic mantle." Milton, in

The Pilgrim of Eternity, whose fame
Over his living head like Heaven is bent,   265
An early but enduring monument,
Came, veiling all the lightnings of his song
In sorrow ; from her wilds Ierne sent
The sweetest lyrist of her saddest wrong,
And love taught grief to fall like music from his tongue.   270

Midst others of less note, came one frail Form,
· A phantom among men ; companionless
As the last cloud of an expiring storm
Whose thunder is its knell ; he, as I guess,
Had gazed on Nature's naked loveliness,   275
Actæon-like, and now he fled astray
With feeble steps o'er the world's wilderness,
And his own thoughts, along that rugged way,
Pursued, like raging hounds, their father and their prey.

A pardlike Spirit beautiful and swift—   280
A Love in desolation masked ;—a Power
Girt round with weakness ;—it can scarce uplift
The weight of the superincumbent hour ;

---

his essay on "Church Government," speaks of the "poet, soaring on the
high reason of his fancies, with his garland and singing robes about him."
  264. **Pilgrim of Eternity**: Byron, who was the Pilgrim of his "Childe
Harold's Pilgrimage."
  267. Shelley misjudged Byron's nature ; he felt no such generous sorrow
as here attributed to him, and wrote a flippant and unfeeling stanza upon
the event in "Don Juan" (xi. 60), which ends with the much quoted lines :

> "Poor fellow ! his was an untoward fate !
> 'Tis strange the mind, that fiery particle,
> Should let itself be snuffed out by an article."

  268. **Ierne** : Ireland, called by the ancients *Iverna, Juverna*, and *Hibernia*.
  269. **Sweetest lyrist** : Thomas Moore, who sang of Ireland's wrongs in
his "Irish Melodies." " Her saddest wrong" may refer to the insurrection of
1803 and the fate of Robert Emmet. See the songs, "Oh, breathe not his
name," "When he who adores thee," and "She is far from the land."
  271. Says Stopford Brooke: "There is nothing in English poetry so steeped
in passionate personality as the description of himself in stanzas xxxi-iv.
It is almost too close, too unveiled, too intense to have been written. The
only other poet—for Byron's self-description is written with a view to effect—
who has approached the wild self-sorrow of it, is Cowper, and he uses the
same simile of the stricken stag."
  276. **Actæon-like** : Actæon, the famous hunter, having come upon Diana
and her nymphs bathing, one day while hunting, was changed into a stag
and torn in pieces by his fifty hounds on Mount Cithæron.

It is a dying lamp, a falling shower,
A breaking billow ;—even whilst we speak 285
Is it not broken ? On the withering flower
The killing sun smiles brightly : on a cheek
  The life can burn in blood, even while the heart may break.

His head was bound with pansies overblown,
And faded violets, white, and pied, and blue ; 290
And a light spear topped with a cypress cone,
Round whose rude shaft dark ivy tresses grew
Yet dripping with the forest's noonday dew,
Vibrated, as the ever-beating heart
Shook the weak hand that grasped it ; of that crew 295
He came the last, neglected and apart ;
  A herd-abandoned deer struck by the hunter's dart.

All stood aloof, and at his partial moan
Smiled through their tears ; well knew that gentle band
Who in another's fate now wept his own ; 300
As in the accents of an unknown land,
He sung new sorrow ; sad Urania scanned
The Stranger's mien, and murmured : " Who art thou ?"
He answered not, but with a sudden hand
Made bare his branded and ensanguined brow, 305
  Which was like Cain's or Christ's—Oh ! that it should be so !

What softer voice is hushed over the dead ?
Athwart what brow is that dark mantle thrown ?
What form leans sadly o'er the white death-bed,
In mockery of monumental stone, 310
The heavy heart heaving without a moan?
If it be He, who, gentlest of the wise,
Taught, soothed, loved, honored the departed one ;
Let me not vex, with inharmonious sighs
  The silence of that heart's accepted sacrifice. 315

---

306. His enemies thought him to be like Cain; his few real friends knew
him to be more like a martyr.
312. The "gentlest of the wise" is Leigh Hunt, one of Keats' earliest and
most faithful friends.

Our Adonais has drunk poison—oh !
What deaf and viperous murderer could crown
Life's early cup with such a draught of woe ?
The nameless worm would now itself disown :
It felt, yet could escape the magic tone   320
Whose prelude held all envy, hate, and wrong,
But what was howling in one breast alone,
Silent with expectation of the song,
Whose master's hand is cold, whose silver lyre unstrung.

Live thou, whose infamy is not thy fame !   325
Live ! fear no heavier chastisement from me,
Thou noteless blot on a remembered name !
But be thyself, and know thyself to be !
And ever at thy season be thou free
To spill the venom when thy fangs o'erflow :   330
Remorse and Self-contempt shall cling to thee ;
Hot Shame shall burn upon thy secret brow,
And like a beaten hound tremble thou shalt—as now.

Nor let us weep that our delight is fled
Far from these carrion kites that scream below ;   335
He wakes or sleeps with the enduring dead ;
Thou canst not soar where he is sitting now.—
Dust to the dust ! but the pure spirit shall flow
Back to the burning fountain whence it came,
A portion of the Eternal, which must glow   340
Through time and change, unquenchably the same,
Whilst thy cold embers choke the sordid hearth of shame.

Peace, peace ! he is not dead, he doth not sleep—
He hath awakened from the dream of life—
'Tis we, who lost in stormy visions, keep   345
With phantoms an unprofitable strife,

---

317. In his preface Shelley thus characterizes the Quarterly reviewer:
"Miserable man! you, one of the meanest, have wantonly defaced one of
the noblest specimens of the workmanship of God. Nor shall it be your ex-
cuse, that murderer as you are, you have spoken daggers but used none."
328. The heaviest curse that can rest upon him is to continue to be the
"viperous" thing that he is, and be conscious of it.
335. **Carrion-kites** : In prose Shelley says of the reviewers of the period :
"They scatter their insults and their slanders without heed as to whether
the poisoned shaft lights on a heart made callous by many blows, or one, like
Keats', composed of more penetrable stuff."

And in mad trance, strike with our spirit's knife
Invulnerable nothings.— *We* decay
Like corpses in a charnel; fear and grief
Convulse us and consume us day by day,   350
And cold hopes swarm like worms within our living clay.

He has outsoared the shadow of our night ;
Envy and calumny and hate and pain,
And that unrest which men miscall delight,
Can touch him not and torture not again ;   355
From the contagion of the world's slow stain
He is secure, and now can never mourn
A heart grown cold, a head grown gray in vain ;
Nor, when the spirit's self has ceased to burn,
With sparkless ashes load an unlamented urn.   360

He lives, he wakes—'tis Death is dead, not he ;
Mourn not for Adonais.—Thou young Dawn
Turn all thy dew to splendor, for from thee
The spirit thou lamentest is not gone ;
Ye caverns and ye forests, cease to moan !   365
Cease ye faint flowers and fountains, and thou Air
Which like a mourning veil thy scarf hadst thrown
O'er the abandoned Earth, now leave it bare
Even to the joyous stars which smile on its despair !

He is made one with Nature : there is heard   370
His voice in all her music, from the moan
Of thunder, to the song of night's sweet bird ;
He is a presence to be felt and known
In darkness and in light, from herb and stone,
Spreading itself where'er that Power may move   375
Which has withdrawn his being to its own :
Which wields the world with never wearied love,
Sustains it from beneath, and kindles it above.

He is a portion of the loveliness
Which once he made more lovely : he doth bear   380
His part, while the one Spirit's plastic stress
Sweeps through the dull dense world, compelling there,

All new successions to the forms they wear ;
Torturing th' unwilling dross that checks its flight
To its own likeness, as each mass may bear ;   385
And bursting in its beauty and its might
From trees and beasts and men into the Heaven's light.

The splendors of the firmament of time
May be eclipsed, but are extinguished not ;
Like stars to their appointed height they climb   390
And death is a low mist which cannot blot
The brightness it may veil. When lofty thought
Lifts a young heart above its mortal lair,
And love and life contend in it, for what
Shall be its earthly doom, the dead live there   395
And move like winds of light on dark and stormy air.

The inheritors of unfulfilled renown
Rose from their thrones, built beyond mortal thought,
Far in the Unapparent.   Chatterton
Rose pale, his solemn agony had not   400
Yet faded from him ; Sidney, as he fought
And as he fell and as he lived and loved
Sublimely mild, a Spirit without spot,
Arose ; and Lucan, by his death approved :
Oblivion as they rose shrank like a thing reproved.   405

And many more, whose names on Earth are dark,
But whose transmitted effluence cannot die
So long as fire outlives the parent spark,
Rose, robed in dazzling immortality.
"Thou art become as one of us," they cry,   410
"It was for thee yon kingless sphere has long
Swung blind in unascended majesty,
Silent alone amid an Heaven of Song.
Assume thy wingèd throne, thou Vesper of our throng !"

---

399. **Chatterton** : Thomas Chatterton, the poet, whom Wordsworth called
"the marvelous boy," and to whose memory Keats dedicated his " Endymion." He was not eighteen when he committed suicide.
 401. **Sidney**: Sir Philip Sidney, poet and " warbler of poetic prose," as
Cowper called him. His friend Spenser described him as " That most heroic
spirit, the heaven's pride, and glory of our day." He died at thirty-two,
from a wound received while aiding the Dutch in their war for independence.
 404. **Lucan**: A Roman poet, whose " Pharsalia " was left unfinished. He

Who mourns for Adonais? oh come forth   415
Fond wretch ! and know thyself and him aright.
Clasp with thy panting soul the pendulous Earth;
As from a center, dart thy spirit's light
Beyond all worlds, until its spacious might
Satiate the void circumference: then shrink   420
Even to a point within our day and night ;
And keep thy heart light lest it make thee sink
When hope has kindled hope, and lured thee to the brink.

Or go to Rome, which is the sepulcher
O, not of him, but of our joy : 'tis naught   425
That ages, empires, and religions there
Lie buried in the ravage they have wrought;
For such as he can lend,—they borrow not
Glory from those who made the world their prey;
And he is gathered to the kings of thought   430
Who waged contention with their time's decay,
And of the past are all that cannot pass away.

Go thou to Rome,—at once the Paradise,
The grave, the city, and the wildnerness ;
And where its wrecks like shattered mountains rise,   435
And flowering weeds, and fragrant copses dress
The bones of Desolation's nakedness
Pass, till the Spirit of the spot shall lead
Thy footsteps to a slope of green access
Where, like an infant's smile, over the dead,   440
A light of laughing flowers along the grass is spread.

---

engaged in a conspiracy against Nero, and on being condemned bled himself
to death.
   417-420. " This seems to mean : Traverse the universe in fancy ; see how
vast it is, what a mere atom of it is this world of ours."—*Prof. Hales.*
   424. Compare with these stanzas Byron's description of Rome—" lone
mother of dead empires," " the Niobe of nations," in " Childe Harold," bk.
IV.
   439. Keats " was buried in the romantic and lonely cemetery of the Protes-
tants in that city. under the pyramid which is the tomb of Cestius, and the
massy walls and towers, now moldering and desolate, which formed the
circuit of ancient Rome. The cemetery is an open space among the ruins,
covered in winter with violets and daisies. It might make one in love with
death to think that one should be buried in so sweet a place."—*Shelley's
Preface.*

And gray walls molder round, on which dull Time
Feeds, like slow fire upon a hoary brand ;
And one keen pyramid with wedge sublime,
Pavilioning the dust of him who planned   445
This refuge for his memory, doth stand
Like flame transformed to marble ; and beneath,
A field is spread, on which a newer band
Have pitched in Heaven's smile their camp of death
Welcoming him we lose with scarce extinguished breath. 450

Here pause : these graves are all too young as yet
To have outgrown the sorrow which consigned
Its charge to each; and if the seal is set,
Here, on one fountain of a mourning mind,
Break it not thou ! too surely shalt thou find   455
Thine own well full, if thou returnest home,
Of tears and gall.   From the world's bitter wind
Seek shelter in the shadow of the tomb.
What Adonais is, why fear we to become ?

The One remains, the many change and pass ;   460
Heaven's light forever shines, Earth's shadows fly ;
Life, like a dome of many-colored glass,
Stains the white radiance of Eternity,
Until Death tramples it to fragments.—Die,
If thou wouldst be with that which thou dost seek !   465
Follow where all is fled !—Rome's azure sky,
Flowers, ruins, statues, music, words, are weak
The glory they transfuse with fitting truth to speak.

Why linger, why turn back, why shrink, my Heart ?
Thy hopes are gone before : from all things here   470
They have departed ; thou shouldst now depart !
A light is past from the revolving year,
And man, and woman ; and what still is dear .

---

449. The cemetery had only recently been made.
462. Like a colored dome through which the true beauty of the skies beyond cannot be seen,
463–465. " Nothing material can adequately express eternal beauty."
473. " There is terrible peril in mutual love, for the loved one may be
lost; also in love which wins no response there is dire distress and pain."—
Prof. Hales.

Attracts to crush, repels to make thee wither.
The soft sky smiles,—the low wind whispers near ;   475
'Tis Adonais calls ! oh, hasten thither,
No more let Life divide what Death can join together.

That Light whose smile kindles the Universe,
That Beauty in which all things work and move,
That Benediction which the eclipsing Curse   480
Of birth can quench not, that sustaining Love
Which through the web of being blindly wove
By man and beast and earth and air and sea,
Burns bright or dim, as each are mirrors of
The fire for which all thirst ; now beams on me,   485
Consuming the last clouds of cold mortality.

The breath whose might I have invoked in song
Descends on me ; my spirit's bark is driven,
Far from the shore, far from the trembling throng
Whose sails were never to the tempest given ;   490
The massy earth and spherèd skies are riven !
I am borne darkly, fearfully, afar;
Whilst burning through the inmost veil of Heaven,
The soul of Adonais, like a star,
Beacons from the abode where the Eternal are.   495

485. **The fire for which all thirst :** The celestial fire, light of eternity.
495. **A few months later, Shelley obeyed the summons.**

ENGLISH CLASSIC SERIES,

FOR

Classes in English Literature, Reading, Grammar, etc.

EDITED BY EMINENT ENGLISH AND AMERICAN SCHOLARS.

Each Volume contains a Sketch of the Author's Life, Prefatory and Explanatory Notes, etc., etc.

(Additional numbers on next page.)

ENGLISH CLASSIC SERIES—CONTINUED.

63 The Antigone of Sophocles. English Version by Thos. Francklin, D.D.
64 Elizabeth Barrett Browning. (Selected Poems.)
65 Robert Browning. (Selected Poems.)
66 Addison, The Spectator. (Sel'ns.)
67 Scenes from George Eliot's Adam Bede.
68 Matthew Arnold's Culture and Anarchy.
69 DeQuincey's Joan of Arc.
70 Carlyle's Essay on Burns.
71 Byron's Childe Harold's Pilgrimage.
72 Poe's Raven, and other Poems.
73 & 74 Macaulay's Lord Clive. (Double Number.)
75 Webster's Reply to Hayne.

76 & 77 Macaulay's Lays of A cient Rome. (Double Numb
78 American Patriotic Selectio Declaration of Independen Washington's Farewell A dress, Lincoln's Gettysb Speech, etc.
79 & 80 Scott's Lady of the La (Condensed.)
81 & 82 Scott's Marmion. ((densed.)
83 & 84 Pope's Essay on Man.
85 Shelley's Skylark, Adonais, other Poems.
86 Dickens's Cricket on Hearth. (In preparation.)
87 Spencer's Philosophy of St (In preparation.)
88 Lamb's Essays of Elia. preparation.)

Single numbers, 32 to 64 pp. Mailing price, 12 cents per copy.
Double numbers, 75 to 128 pp. Mailing price, 24 cents per cop

SPECIAL PRICES TO TEACHERS.

SPECIAL NUMBERS.

Milton's Paradise Lost. Book I. With portrait and graphical sketch of Milton, essay on his genius, epitome of the views of the I known critics, Milton's verse, argument, and full introductory and explana notes. Bound in boards. *Mailing price, 30 cents.*

Milton's Paradise Lost. Books I. and II. With portrait biographical sketch of Milton, his verse; essay on his genius, epitome of the v of the best-known critics, argument, and full introductory and explanatory n Bound in boards. *Mailing price, 40 cents.*

Wykes's Shakespeare Reader. Being extracts from Plays of Shakespeare, with introductory paragraphs, and grammatical, histor and explanatory notes. By C. H. WYKES. 160 pp., 16mo, cloth. *Mailing p 35 cents.*

Chaucer's The Canterbury Tales. The Prologue. text collated with the seven oldest MSS., a portrait and biographical sketch o author, introductory notices, grammar, critical and explanatory notes, inde obsolete and difficult words, argument and characters of the prologue, brief his of English language to time of Chaucer, and glossary. Bound in boards. *Ma price, 35 cents.*

Chaucer's The Squieres Tale. With portrait and biogr. ical sketch of author, introduction to his grammar and versification, glossar amination papers, and full explanatory notes. Bound in boards. *Mailing 35 cents.*

Chaucer's The Knightes Tale. With portrait and graphical sketch of author, essay on his language, history of the English lan to time of Chaucer, glossary, and full explanatory notes. Bound in boards. *ing price, 40 cents.*

Goldsmith's She Stoops to Conquer. With biograp sketch of author, introduction, dedication, Garrick's Prologue, epilogue and intended epilogues, and full explanatory notes. Bound in boards. *Mailing 30 cents.*

FULL DESCRIPTIVE CATALOGUE SENT ON APPLICATION.

www.ingramcontent.com/pod-product-compliance
Lightning Source LLC
Chambersburg PA
CBHW030903260626
47169CB00008B/2663